Jolly Old Santa Claus

Jolly Old Santa Claus

COLLECTOR'S EDITION FEATURING
THE ORIGINAL STORY BY "SPARKIE"
WITH THE CLASSIC OIL PAINTINGS BY
GEORGE HINKE

CandyCane Press
AN IMPRINT OF
IDEALS PUBLICATIONS INCORPORATED
NASHVILLE, TENNESSEE

Mrs. Santa Claus

Whiskers

*Chief
Elf*

*Gram'pa
Elf*

Published by Ideals Publications Incorporated
535 Metroplex Drive, Nashville, Tennessee 37211

Printed and bound in Mexico

ISBN 0-8249-4080-6

The display type is set in Linoscript.
The text type is set in Bernhard Modern.
Color separations by Precision Color Graphics, New Berlin, Wisconsin.
Printed and bound by RR Donnelley & Sons
DESIGNED BY JOY CHU

Second edition
10 8 6 4 2   3 5 7 9

A Historical Note

Jasper
Elf

Jeepers
Elf

Jehoshaphat
Elf

Jingles
Elf

Junior
Elf

JOLLY OLD SANTA CLAUS, *whose author was known only as "Sparkie," was first published by Ideals magazine in 1961. Although the original edition has been out of print for several years, old and worn copies are still being read to children by adults who heard the story from their parents. We are proud to republish this collector's edition featuring the finely crafted oil paintings by George Hinke along with the original prose story.*

George Hinke was born in Berlin, Germany, in 1883 and schooled in a classic style of painting. Mr. Hinke came to Milwaukee, Wisconsin, in 1923, where he worked at a printing shop until he opened his own studio. From 1944 until Mr. Hinke's death in 1953, Ideals commissioned him to create many works of art. In addition to Santa Claus, Mr. Hinke's subjects included American small-town life, American flags, and religious scenes—all in his classic, nostalgic style.

The paintings in JOLLY OLD SANTA CLAUS *are rendered in oil on stretched canvas. The influence of Mr. Hinke's German background is evident in the Santa Claus series: from Santa's castle, which resembles the castles of Bavarian kings, to the Black Forest clock on the wall of Santa's workshop to the elves themselves, who are reminiscent of those characters in stone that decorate many German gardens.*

Ideals Publications Incorporated is pleased to share these delightful and masterful paintings with a new generation of children. We have no doubt that Mr. Hinke would be proud of this exquisite collector's edition of JOLLY OLD SANTA CLAUS.

"Ho, ho!"

"Ho, ho!" laughed Jolly Old Santa Claus as he stroked his long white beard. He chuckled again, his eyes twinkling and merry.

"Come, my hardworking elves. Come, my dear Mrs. Santa," he called. "Come listen to this very wonderful letter."

Mrs. Santa Claus was playing the piano while Santa's elves were singing Christmas carols. They stopped and all came over to Santa.

"What does it say?" "Who is it from?" "Did a little boy or a little girl write it?" "Where is it from? Did the . . ."

"Whoa there, just a moment, my fine friends," said Jolly Old Santa Claus. "One question at a time!"

"It is a letter from a little boy who has been very good all year. He has minded his mommy and his daddy. He has helped his brothers and his sister. He has been kind to his little dog. But can you guess what he wants to know?"

The elves all tried to guess.

"Will he get a train for Christmas?" "Will you find his new house?" "Will it snow on Christmas Eve?"

"No, no—you'll never guess," chuckled Santa Claus. "This good little boy wants to know if we are busy getting ready for Christmas!"

"We most certainly are!" shouted Santa's elves.

The North Pole is the busiest place in the world just before Christmas.

Santa and his elves are working hard, baking cookies and making wonderful toys for all the boys and girls.

Would you like a tour of Santa's workshops at the North Pole? Let's follow Jolly Old Santa Claus as he prepares for Christmas Eve. We must be very quiet, though. If we disturb Santa and his elves, they will never finish their work by midnight on Christmas Eve.

I smell cookies. Santa must be heading for the

Cookie Kitchen.

Just look

at the elves scurrying about, with great smudges of flour on their aprons and sugar on their hands. How hard they are working!

Oops! Watch out Gram'pa Elf! The sacks of flour are heavy! Just look at Gram'pa. He never remembers to wear his spectacles.

Do you see Jeepers Elf, sitting on top of the oven? He's telling the other elves how to place the trays of cookies so they won't burn.

Star-shaped cookies, heart-shaped cookies, gingerbread cookies, round and fat little cookies—dozens and dozens of cookies for the good girls and boys.

It looks like they are having such fun making cookies. Do you like to make Christmas cookies?

Let's hurry on. Santa's North Pole is a big place,

and there is so much

more to see.

Jolly Old Santa Claus is going outside to check on the work there. He has just asked Chief Elf if the Christmas trees are all ready.

Christmas trees grow all over the forest. Won't they look lovely after Jolly Old Santa Claus and his helpers have decorated them with pretty glass ornaments?

The little animals love to watch the elves, because they whistle and sing while they work. If you listen closely when you walk in the forest, you might hear their singing too.

Did you see old Gram'pa Elf slip in the deep snow? He's lost his cap! He's the funniest elf, isn't he? He just never remembers to wear those spectacles!

I wonder where Jeepers Elf is. He's probably talking to the reindeer. Do you see him?

It won't be long now before Santa Claus will be ready to leave the North Pole, and then it will almost be

Christmastime.

Why, here is Jolly Old Santa's office! It must be—for look! There is his desk and there is Santa Claus, reading the letters from boys and girls all over the world.

On the wall hangs his list of good little boys and girls and bad little boys and girls. Oh, no! Junior Elf is putting a mark under "Bad Little Boys and Girls." I'm sure it's not for you!

Mrs. Santa Claus is marking the names and addresses of all little boys and girls who have moved to new houses since last year, so Jolly Old Santa Claus will be sure to find them.

Do you see Whiskers the cat sitting on top of Santa's chair? And just look at Jehoshaphat Elf taking a break under Santa's desk.

Jasper Elf and Jeepers Elf are opening letters for Santa to read. There's Jingles Elf. He's supervising the delivery of the huge, heavy sack of letters. Have you ever seen so many letters?

Santa Claus looks happy. Do you think he's reading a letter from a very good little boy or girl?

Let's follow Santa to the Christmas Tree Ornament Shop.

Look at the fires in the furnace! That is where the elves melt the glass that they blow into Christmas tree ornaments. It looks like they are blowing colorful soap bubbles.

Have you ever seen so many bright and shiny ornaments?

Some elves are dipping the ornaments into paint while other elves are using brushes to paint. There's Jingles helping to box the glass ornaments.

Making ornaments is a very special job. Only the most careful elf can work here, for the glass ornaments have to be handled very carefully or they will break. Uh oh! Junior Elf just kicked over a box of glass balls. He has a lot of cleaning up to do!

Do you see Whiskers? She's sitting up on top of the furnace out of the way. If she walked on the floor, her long tail might break the ornaments, and Chief Elf wouldn't like that at all!

There's Jasper Elf. He's sitting up high on top of the tool shelf, watching Jolly Old Santa Claus admire the beautiful ornaments.

It's getting closer and closer to

Christmastime!

Let's hurry on to the best place in the world! Let's go to Santa's

Toy Shop!

Did you think Santa's Toy Shop would look like this? All the elves are so busy. All of them, that is, except Junior Elf. Just look at him—riding the rock-a-bye pony when he should be painting toys.

Jolly Old Santa Claus is checking his list of toys. He's got airplanes, trains, drums, building blocks, dolls, teddy bears, bouncing balls, and candy canes. Which toy do you like best? Do you think he has enough toys for all the boys and girls all around the world? Does he have enough toys for you?

There's Whiskers again. She's always close to Jolly Old Santa. Do you see Gram'pa Elf falling down the stairs? I think old Jack-in-the-box frightened him, don't you?

Look at the clock on the wall! It's almost midnight on Christmas Eve.

Chief Elf has seen the clock too. He's telling all the elves to hurry. They still must finish painting all the toys, and it's getting very late.

Now it's almost time for Santa to begin his trip. Everyone has a job. His elves are loading the sleigh. Mrs. Claus is making certain that Jolly Old Santa Claus will leave exactly at midnight. Jehoshaphat Elf is in charge of Santa's address list so that he will know where the reindeer must stop. Junior Elf harnesses the reindeer to the sleigh. And look what Mrs. Santa Claus is holding—earmuffs and a heavy scarf, so Santa will be warm tonight.

For it is coming tonight. Tonight is the night of all nights. Tonight is

the night before Christmas!

Swiftly through the skies Santa and his reindeer will fly. More quietly than falling snow, he will land atop your house. Then silently—oh, so silently—down your chimney he will come. He will fill your stocking with goodies. He may trim your tree with ornaments. And underneath the tree, what wonderful surprises there will be!

Then just as quietly—and just as quickly as he came—he will be gone.

Jolly Old Santa Claus will work all through the night, bringing happiness and joy and love into the homes of all good little boys and girls.

And long before the sun rises in the Christmas morning sky,

Jolly Old

Santa Claus

will visit the homes of every good little boy and girl all over the world and be on his way back to the North Pole.

Upon Santa's return, Mrs. Claus and all the elves

greet him with such
excitement!

They are all eager to ask Jolly Old Santa about his trip.

"Did it snow, Santa Claus?"

"Was it very cold?"

"Were the good little boys and girls all fast asleep in their beds?"

Look at Whiskers! What a wonderful Christmas gift she gives Jolly Old Santa Claus: four soft, cuddly baby kittens.

After the reindeer are unhitched and fed, Jolly Old Santa Claus goes into his house and takes off his coat and boots. Junior Elf brings his slippers. Mrs. Santa Claus serves hot chocolate and cookies to Santa, who is very glad to be home on this

wonderful Christmas Day!

But the elves still have much work to do. Jingles Elf offers to shine Santa's boots and polish the sleigh bells.

First the elves finish cleaning the workshops. Tools are put back in their places. Spilled paint is wiped up, and unused toys are packed away for use next year. After the cleanup is finished,

what do Santa's elves do?

They eat Mrs. Claus's cookies, drink some milk, and head for bed for a long night's sleep.

How tired they all are. Jolly Old Santa Claus, Mrs. Claus, and all Santa's elves have worked very hard baking Christmas cookies, collecting trees, painting beautiful ornaments, making wonderful toys, and getting everything ready for you on Christmas morning.

After the elves are in bed, Santa and Mrs. Claus tiptoe upstairs. Standing at the top of the winding staircase, they softly call "good night" to all the elves.

And if you listen very closely, you might hear the elves and Mrs. Santa Claus and Jolly Old Santa Claus softly call to every good little boy and good little girl everywhere,

"Happy Christmas to all, and to all a good night!"